The Biggest Pest
on Eighth Avenue

The Biggest Pest on Eighth Avenue

by Laurie Lawlor

illustrated by Cynthia Fisher

Holiday House/New York

For my brother Tom—from Eighth Avenue
to Broadway
L. L.
To Fran and Hank
C. F.

Text copyright © 1997 by Laurie Lawlor
Illustrations copyright © 1997 by Cynthia Fisher
ALL RIGHTS RESERVED
Printed in the United States of America
FIRST EDITION

Library of Congress Cataloging-in-Publication Data
Lawlor, Laurie.
The Biggest Pest on Eighth Avenue / by Laurie Lawlor ;
illustrated by Cynthia Fisher.
p.   cm.
Summary: An amateur horror show scares no one except its creators
until a frightful actor appears on the scene.
ISBN 0-8234-1321-7 (reinforced)
[1. Plays—Fiction.   2. Brothers and sisters—Fiction.]
I. Fisher, Cynthia, ill.   II. Title.
PZ7.L4189Sc   1997   97-2215   CIP   AC
[E]—dc21

Contents

1. Nothing But a Pest

Leo tossed his jaunty scarf
over one shoulder,
just like a real director.
"Your garage," he told Mary Lou,
"is just the place for us
    to perform the scariest play
    ever seen on Eighth Avenue."
Mary Lou smiled with pride.
"My father never parks the car
    in here.
No grownups will bother us,"
    she promised.
"There's plenty of room
    in the driveway for the audience,"
Leo said. "And just imagine
this doorway with a stage curtain.
It's perfect!"

6

"When do we start?"

Mary Lou asked eagerly.

"Just as soon as you tell
   your terrible brother to get down
   off the roof," Leo replied.
   Sure enough, there was Tommy
   perched on the roof.
"Tommy!" Mary Lou shouted.
"What do you think you're doing?"
"I'm practicing being the Face
   on the Bedroom Curtain Who
   Peers at You While You Sleep,"
   Tommy said.
"Can I be in your scary play?"

"Absolutely not," Mary Lou replied.

"You are nothing but a pest.

Get down this instant."

But Tommy refused to budge.

Mary Lou sighed.

"Just ignore him," she told Leo

in a voice loud enough

for Tommy to hear.

"We have important work to do."

She and Leo dragged wagons
and bikes from the garage. They
lined up chairs, benches, and boxes
in the driveway for the audience.
Sometimes, when Leo wasn't looking,
Mary Lou looked up.
Tommy was still perched on the roof,
motionless as a curtain
on a windless night.

2.   The Haunted Castle of Doom

Lynn lived next door.

When she noticed the rows of

chairs, benches, and boxes

in the driveway,

she knew something exciting

and theatrical was about to happen

in Mary Lou's garage.

Lynn pushed a big box of dress-up

clothes down Mary Lou's driveway.

"I bet you can use these

in your play," she said.

"Perfect!" exclaimed Leo.

"And this box is just what we need
for the Haunted Castle of Doom,"
Mary Lou said.
While Mary Lou painted the castle,
Lynn and Leo created
a fabulous stage curtain.

12

Mary Lou was so busy, she forgot
about her terrible brother.
"Oh no!" she whispered
when she looked at the roof.
"Where did he go?"
"Who cares?" Leo replied.
"What if he's hurt?" Mary Lou said.
"Nothing," said Leo,
"can hurt that pest."

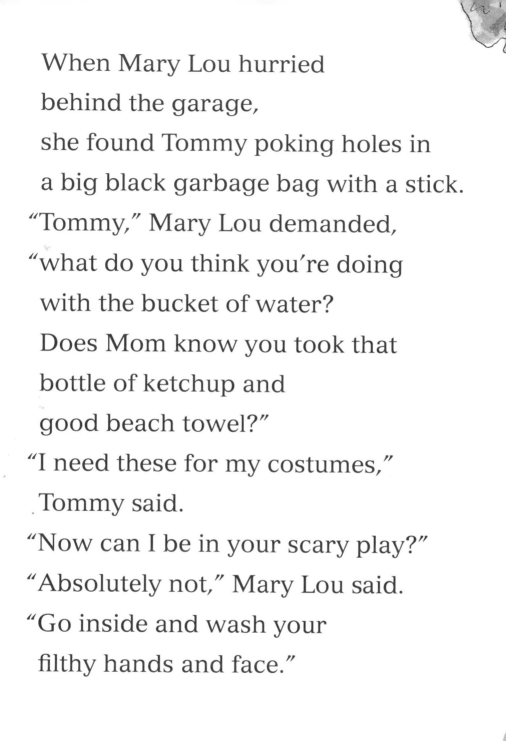

When Mary Lou hurried
behind the garage,
she found Tommy poking holes in
a big black garbage bag with a stick.
"Tommy," Mary Lou demanded,
"what do you think you're doing
with the bucket of water?
Does Mom know you took that
bottle of ketchup and
good beach towel?"
"I need these for my costumes,"
Tommy said.
"Now can I be in your scary play?"
"Absolutely not," Mary Lou said.
"Go inside and wash your
filthy hands and face."

3. AAAAEEEEEYAH!

Mary Lou trudged back
inside the garage.
"How do you like my
Evil Queen crown?" Lynn asked.
Mary Lou frowned.
While she was busy Lynn had
grabbed the best dress-up outfit.

"It's time to advertise," Leo said.
  He retied his jaunty scarf.
"We need to make lots of posters.
  We need to sell lots of tickets.
  We have to let everyone know
  that this is going to be
  the scariest play ever seen on
  Eighth Avenue."

Mary Lou and Lynn marched up
and down the block.
"How can I be sure
you're telling the truth?"
a neighbor boy asked.
"I don't want to waste
my money if your show
isn't *very* scary."
Mary Lou thought hard.

"If you're not scared out of your wits,"
  she said, "we'll give you
  your money back."
"You will?" he demanded.
"And don't forget about the popcorn,"
  Lynn said and winked. "It's free
  and you can eat all you want."
The boy smacked his lips
  and ran to tell his friends.

When Mary Lou and Lynn returned
to the driveway,
Leo had artistically created
a mountain of tickets.
"I hope a lot of people come,"
Lynn said.

"Shouldn't we rehearse?"
Mary Lou asked.
Before Leo could answer,
a terrible terrifying cry
filled the air. "AAAAEEEEEYAH!"
"Who's that?" Lynn asked fearfully.
Mary Lou ran inside the house.
She opened the bathroom door.

There was Tommy standing
in the toilet in his red sneakers.
Flushing water swirled
around his ankles.
"AHEEEEEEEYAH!" he cried.
"It's cold in here!"
"What do you think
you're doing?" Mary Lou demanded.
"Practicing the part
of the Angry
Alligator Who Sneaks
Down the Sewer Pipe,"
he said.

"Now can I be in your scary play?"

"Absolutely not.

You are nothing but a pest,"
she said. "Dry yourself off."
She pulled him out of the toilet
and hurried outside.

4. The Murky Dark Dangerous Forest

"Be sure to paint every tree in
the Murky Dark Dangerous Forest,"
Leo insisted.
Mary Lou sighed.

Her hands were green.

Her arms were green.

Her face was green—

even her teeth were green.

"When do we rehearse?"

Mary Lou asked. She watched

Lynn try on the

Evil Queen's spiky crown

for the hundredth time.

She gave Lynn an evil look.

"I'll decide when we rehearse,"

said Leo. "I'm the director."

"What if the forest doesn't dry

in time?" Mary Lou said.

"The show must go on," Leo replied.

Suddenly, a terrible terrifying cry

filled the air. "AAAAEEEEEYAH!"

Not again!

Mary Lou checked the roof.

She ran inside the house.

No Tommy.

She checked the bathroom.

No Tommy.

She opened the bedroom door

and there was Tommy

wedged up to his armpits

inside the clothes chute.

"AAAAAHEEEEEYAH!" he cried.

"It's tight in here!"

"What do you think you're doing?"

Mary Lou demanded.

"Practicing how fast I can

escape down the trap door

of the Haunted Castle of Doom.

Now can I be in your scary play?"

"Absolutely not.

Stop bothering us and

stay out of trouble,"

she said and pulled him out

of the clothes chute.

Mary Lou hurried to the garage.

It was almost one o'clock.

At this rate, they'd never be ready.

"We forgot to make popcorn,"
Lynn moaned.

"Better get some ready," Leo said.
Meanwhile, he and Mary Lou
struggled to collect the tickets that
had blown all over the yard.

"Help me put the curtain back up,"
Leo said. His face was red.
His scarf did not look
jaunty anymore.

"Here's the popcorn," Lynn said.

"Just in time!" Mary Lou exclaimed.

The audience had begun to line up
in the driveway.

"We haven't rehearsed!"

Mary Lou whispered frantically.

"The show must go on,"
said Leo. He retied his scarf.

He looked like his old self again.

"Costumes, everyone!"

Mary Lou pulled on a knight's helmet,
football pads and an evening gown.

"Who are you supposed to be?"

Lynn demanded.

Mary Lou stared at the paint
on her hands and arms.

"I'm the Great Green
   Warrior Princess," she replied.
"Oh," said Lynn. She placed the
   Evil Queen's spiky crown on her head
   and smiled at her reflection
   in the window glass.

5. The Show Must Go On

"We want the show!

We want the show!"

the audience jeered.

They stomped their feet.

They threw popcorn.

"Places, everyone!"

Leo said nervously.

"Remember, be scary!"

He opened the curtain.

Mary Lou held her breath offstage.

She felt too afraid to be in the scariest

play ever seen on Eighth Avenue.

"Where is my daughter,

the Great Green Warrior Princess?"

the Evil Queen cackled.

"I am going to feed her to

wild ferocious dogs in the dungeon."

The Evil Queen opened the dungeon.

CLUNK!

The Haunted Castle of Doom collapsed.

So did the Murky Dark
Dangerous Forest.

The audience hooted.

"This isn't very scary!"

"I want my money back!"

"Go out there, Mary Lou!"

Leo hissed from backstage.

"I can't," she whimpered.

Her feet were stuck to the ground

like soft, pink bubble gum

on a hot summer day.

A terrible
terrifying cry
filled the air.
"AAAAAHHH-
HHEEEEEYAH!"
Everyone
looked up.

Nobody expected the crumpled
black garbage bag on the roof
to suddenly spring to life and shout,
"Beware the hungry Creature
from the Black Magoo!"
The audience gasped.
The Creature from the Black Magoo
growled and wiggled his fingers.
"Look!" someone shouted. "Bloody hands!"
"Does he eat people?"
Two little girls started to cry.
The Creature from the Black Magoo
leapt into the air and scurried across
the garage roof to the tree.

"Where'd that scary monster go?"
  the audience shouted.
"Keep those bloody hands
  away from me!"
"AAAAAHHHHHEEEEEYAH!"
  To everyone's surprise,
  the terrible terrifying voice
  came from behind the garage.
  Tommy darted toward the driveway
  wearing his mother's best beach towel.
"Sewer pipe explosion!" he shouted.

WHOOSH! He splashed the audience
with water from the bucket.
"Don't worry! The Angry Alligator
Who Sneaks Down the Sewer Pipe
will save you!"
And as quickly as he had appeared,
the Angry Alligator scurried
behind the garage again.
"Yuck!" shrieked someone.
"Was that really sewer water?"

"AAAAAHHHHHEEEEEYAH!"

The Creature from the Black Magoo

howled atop the garage roof.

"I must escape that Angry Alligator

Who Sneaks Down the Sewer Pipe.

I know! I'll jump through

the trap door into the dungeon

of the Haunted Castle of Doom!"

The Creature from the Black Magoo

pranced, twirled, and vanished.

For several moments,

not a sound was heard.

Bravely, the Great Green
Warrior Princess
announced in her loudest voice,
"After the wild ferocious dogs
caught up with the Creature
in the dungeon,
he was never seen again. The end!"
The audience cheered.

6. Bravo!

Leo pulled the curtain shut.

"Curtain call," he hissed.

Tommy scrambled down
the tree behind the garage.
Leo opened the curtain.

On stage stepped the Great Green
Warrior Princess,
the Evil Queen and, of course,
the Creature from the Black Magoo.

They bowed and bowed.

The audience went wild.

"Bravo!

Bravo!"

Everyone clapped and whistled.

Leo shut the curtain.

"Great show!" he said.

"That *was* the scariest play
ever seen on Eighth Avenue!"

"Thanks to you, Tommy," said Lynn.

"Maybe you're not such a pest
after all," admitted Mary Lou.

"Our next play is going to be
even scarier. We'll call it
'King Cobra Night Stalker
from the Black Magoo',"
announced Leo. He tossed his
jaunty scarf over one shoulder.

"Of course, you'll be in our show,
won't you, Tommy?"

"Absolutely!" Tommy replied.

With a grin on his face,
he hurried inside the house
to practice slithering head first
down the stairway.